Always Olivia

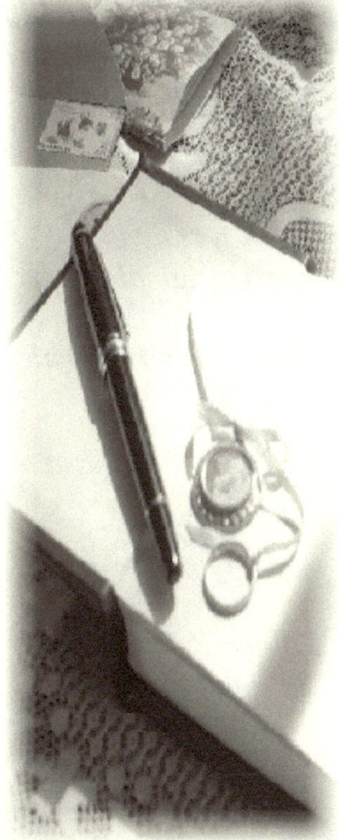

Written By Alex McLellan

2nd Edition 2020 By Author
ISBN : 978-1-989887-07-3

Always Olivia Is
A Forest Original Product
&
A Small Potato Production

1st Edition Printed in 2008
By Publish America
Baltimore, USA
ISBN: 1-60610-143-9

I dedicate this book to our children,
Amelia & Nathan
With love.

Contents

Introduction

Introduction

Always Olivia is sequel to The Memoirs of Mrs. Olivia Foxworthy and is the book many had been waiting for in its 1st Edition .
So dear to my heart now, Olivia has become a real sense of strength for me and in sharing her life adventure, I hope many more will benefit from her. A fictitious character, still I have found myself wondering many times, "What would Olivia do in my situation?" Those moments of pondering have saved me grief on more than one occasion.
I hope all enjoy this heartfelt journey as our heroine continues to be the best she can be. Her legacy spans lifetimes, defies logic and even tempts the most faithful to question their beliefs in a good way. As in life,

Olivia's ups and downs are situations we can all relate to, feel, and learn from. So put your feet up, and fall into the life and times of Mrs. Olivia Foxworthy in its 2nd Edition, and please enjoy, Always Olivia.

~Alex McLellan

Always Olivia
Family Note:

"Thanks to all who enjoyed my Momma's first book, The Memoirs of Mrs. Olivia Foxworthy. She opened up a world so special to so many of us.

I'd like to take the opportunity to mention, my brothers and I read every letter sent to us.

When a person writes their memoirs, especially in the manner Momma did, leaving them all over the house, there is no guarantee some day when you least expect it, others will turn up.

Well years have passed since publishing the first book, and we thought that just might be all there was. We should have had a little faith.

As Momma would say, "It just wasn't the right time yet and all truths will eventually find the light of day...Just like small potatoes. And we all know that big things can come from small potatoes!"

Well, my Clara, the one who laughs "The Laugh" must have needed a little something from her grandmother.

When the time was right, it would be Clara to hold in her hand a journal that changed all the lives of our family, and a family of strangers would be forever bound to us by a mutual honor and devotion.

After discovering the journal, my brothers and I decided Clara would have to decide what would happen next, just as Momma had requested. It was a huge responsibility and we know God works in mysterious ways but this time, angels must have walked beside her.

And so, once again, my rainy day happened. When all was said and done, everyone involved agreed, book two was in the works. Every time, we think of all that has happened, when we lay blame, try to find fault, realize the good, remember the best of the best, we feel all roads lead to Momma. Yes indeed, it's Always Olivia."
Abigail Foxworthy-Johnson

Chapter One: Trunks & Treasures

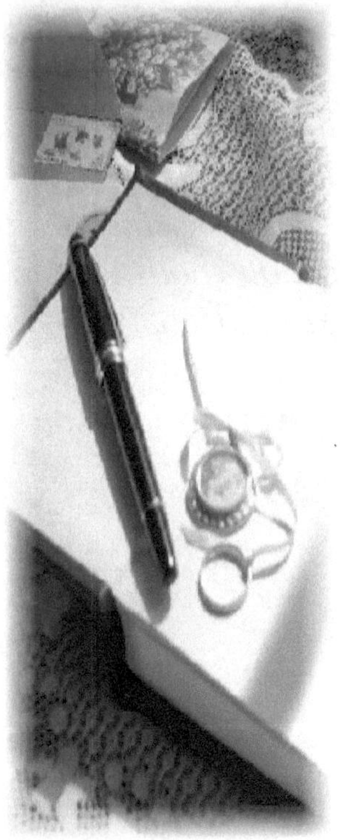

Chapter One:
Trunks & Treasures

It wasn't until her first big move that my Clara would find the need for that old trunk. To think of what happened next is almost too much to take in. Momma must be somewhere really enjoying herself at our expense this time, and I mean that in a good way. It's really a difficult thing for my brothers and I to raise our children without our mother in our lives. We published her words and all the kids have a "feel" regarding what kind of person she was, but as life's lessons touch our children, and they grow older, my brothers and I find we could really use Momma's help from time to time. Sometimes, our children yearn for something they think is missing in their lives, answers to questions that only living life can give and they simply have to do the time to get there.

We were moving only across the city, but to Clara, we were worlds away. A new neighborhood, new friends, a new life and a fourteen-year old who thought she knew everything, except the answer to why she was cross a lot of the time.

As parents, we can try to understand, but until we walk in their shoes, we don't know how life actually is for them. Sometimes, I remember thinking I had more in common with my grandparents, than I had in common with my own daughter.

Well, it was her time now, and it was my Momma who saw to it.

Clara was very excited to get hold of that old trunk. Momma always told her that one day it would be hers and it was a very special trunk. Clara loved it because it held sweet memories of her and Momma. She loved Momma. They had something special. My Mother never played favorites but she and Clara always seemed similar somehow and no one minded. In typical Clara fashion, she was moving that trunk with or without help and she and her mop head of big curls started pull'n that trunk down the stairs one step at a time.

I had been in the kitchen making a pot of coffee. It was my turn to clean up Momma's house and that's when I heard that racket coming down the stairs.

"Clara is that necessary? Let me give you a hand."

As I came around the corner, I could see Clara was beginning to cry.

"Well, you could have waited. I was right around the corner. Are you hurt?"

"No." Clara's eyes looked to the trunk. It appeared broken until I got closer.

"Oh – Oh! You grab that handle and head right back upstairs, young lady!"

"I didn't mean to break it, honest!"

"Oh my, Lord! You little, Monkey! Look at this!"

"Ah, C'mon, Mom! I really didn't mean it!"

"Clara, look honey!"

We stood in Momma's bedroom and then we sat crossed legged on the floor. "Well, this is too good to be true, are you ready? What do you think is in it?"

"I don't know, Mom. This is so amazing!"

We had discovered a false bottom. That trunk I used to keep my dress up clothes in and played with it every day, and I never even once suspected. The silence was almost deafening. It was like finding buried treasure. Right on top, a beautiful piece of fabric and a letter to Clara. Tempting as it was to rifle through all the stuff, I stood up and looked down at my daughter.
"Clara, obviously your grandmother had something she wanted to share with you." Clara's eyes were huge with suspense.
"I'll be in the kitchen. Take as long as you like. Then please, please, please show me what you found?" I begged my teenager.
"O.k. Mom." She looked a little scared.
I closed the door and I could see she was nervous. I couldn't help giggling

a little. I couldn't imagine what was in there, under that cloth. Guess I would have to wait. It was Clara's moment now. This was just the sort of thing I was hoping for, Clara's rainy day, and I whispered, "Are we having fun yet, Momma? Thanks."
Clara slowly opened the letter.

"Dear Clara,
Guess you must be pretty grown by now and guess I'll never know when you'll find this. I'll have to have faith it's the right time. I wanted to leave this old trunk to you because we enjoyed our time together playing in it with your toys and I hope it will be special to you as it is to me.
Clara, there are some occasions in life where a person might just not know where they belong. A person

can get to thinking they are in the wrong place and everything about that place feels wrong. I can tell you honestly that's how it is because I felt that way on more than one occasion and the only comfort is knowing there is a bigger plan, bigger than you, bigger than me, God inspired it must be, but it's there and one day, you will feel it and then you will know for certain, I speak the truth.

As I write to you, and well, you're just a wiper snapper of a child now, I do not know what the future holds or how long I will be on this earth. I know one thing, and that is I love you dearly and if I could walk with you a while, say something should happen to me and I pass away, I would walk with you if I could get there, I swear. I love you that much, child.

When you lift this cloth, you will find a journal from someone I loved more than my own life. It's not mine and I'm pretty sure if I'm not around, you will have heard his name.
This type of love is very rare and hard to imagine at the best of times, but I swear I lived it, young one. When you read the words, please keep me close. I read them many times over and should have reacted differently perhaps, but I was young, and times were very different then. I trust you with my most valuable possession. Not a person, but a love, a great love. Not time, racism, hatred, society, not even my own mother could beat this from my heart. This kind of love is part of a person's being and not to be messed with, if you catch my meaning. Tread carefully sweetest of hearts. Decisions made will change lives.

You must feel you are doing right with every inch of who you are. Your wide eyes are like my Sweetest of Angels, little Hattie. She is someone you never knew. Please see life for the wonder it is for the both of you. It's no small task I am asking but I always have had a faith so strong in people, I truly believe my trust in you will not be for noth'n. That's how much I love yah. Love Gramma Olivia"

"Mom!!! I can't do this! Mom! Something bad will happen if I read this stuff!"
I ran to Clara. "What are you going on about?"
"Gramma Olivia wrote me a letter when I was little and it reads like she's right here, sitting on the bed!

I'm scared! What if I screw up? She writes there are decisions to be made? What do I do?"
"Do you trust Gramma?"
"Yah," Clara answered sheepishly.
"Read!"
Well Clara never did open the door for some time. Hours passed and when she came out, she was a changed person. I hadn't seen her like that since she was very little and when the door finally opened, I was waiting to find out what there was new to know. I sat on the top stair and was prompt to ask many questions, and then I saw her face.
She had been crying.
"Clara?"
"It'll be o.k. Mom. There is much work to be done. Can you come with me into the back yard?"

"Sure honey, but what is this all about?"
"You'll see in a minute."
We walked to the back yard. We went to a tree in the right hand corner. Clara looked to the sun for a moment and felt the sun on her face with her eyes closed. She breathed in deeply and then turned towards the house. The basement part of the house was made of old stone and cement. Clara counted five up and five across from the corner of the house at the height where the sun was hitting her face when she stood by the tree, and the stone came loose.
Behind a special stone was a small hole in the house and she pulled out a tiny tin box. She opened the box and within it, a very small skeleton key. She took the key and headed back into

the house. Was it the key to a trunk that was never locked? I was shocked.
"Well, you having any fun yet? Let's go!"
I followed my only child back into my mother's house and up the stairs.
We sat together on the floor at the trunk and Clara became very serious.
"Mom, Gramma is trusting some huge big stuff to me and I better take it seriously. My first decision is to let you in on all of this."
"Thank you, I'm sure."
"We're gonna need bus tickets."
"I should have guessed as much."
"And we're gonna need'm soon."
"Where are we headed?"
"We're go'n to Jedidiah and Olivia Country," Clara locked the trunk and wore the key around her neck on a string.
"Oh, I see. Let the adventure begin!"

Chapter Two
Righting Wrongs

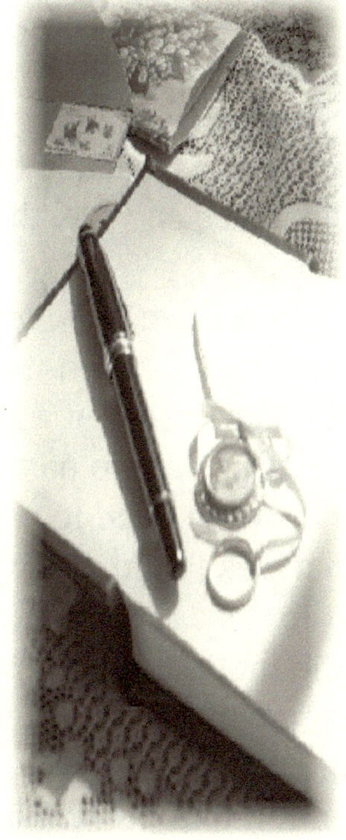

Chapter Two
Righting Wrongs

It was now Clara's time to live as we had lived, wrapped in a life discovering a reality outside ourselves and learning to see and feel through another's eyes.

I trusted Clara and we were on a bus that very weekend. I called it an adventure and she called it a road trip. We had over six hours to pass together and she decided to share a little of what was found and what we were about to do.

That was the first moment I ever knew about my mother's deceit. I was devastated. I felt like she never loved my father. I felt like my whole life was a lie. Clara, in her fourteen years of earthly wisdom reminded me about time and to give the situation some of it, and to have a little faith. I felt the advice was condescending, but tried to stay focused on the task at hand, which I didn't even know what that was by the way.

So there I was on a God forsaken bus with my daughter, going who knows where, completely disappointed in my mother who I had revered as a saint. Clara looked at me, she saw my disappointment and then started to cry.

"Do you still love Gramma even though I told you how much she loved Jedidiah Brown?"

"Well, of course, we read her memoirs. I just didn't realize how much she loved him I guess. I'm just disappointed because I'm trying to figure out where Grampa fit into all this."

Clara reached into her back pack and pulled out a tattered old book. Well, it looked more like a stack of old papers bound with two old book backs and a thin old leather belt, and it smelled bad.

“Look real close.” She pointed to the top right hand corner.

I read the name, “Jedidiah Brown.”

“Clara, are you about to tell me these tattered old sheets belonged to Jedidiah Brown?”

“He was a really good man, Mom. Wait till you read.”

“But where did it come from? I always thought they loved each other as children and never met again.”

“Not true and now I am supposed to let you read a memoir from Gramma.” She handed me the memoir from my mother.

"About My Love,

Today was a day I will always remember. I am entrusting a very special task to a small child who I believe in to set things right one day. I can never share this with my beloved Emery as he is gone now, but I pray that he will know somehow. Love can be a strange and powerful force in the world. It's the kind of thing I can barely believe, so strange.
Today I received a letter from a friend of Emery's in the war. Well, it was addressed to Emery and I opened it. It was from an old man who wrote to Emery to get something off his chest before he died. Guess he and Emery fought together, and I recall the letter remarked about the time black men were commissioned to fight, some were even sold as slaves to fight on

their owners behalf. Some states were more progressive than others, but most of the world was filled with ignorance back then.

I remember Emery mentioning to me in a letter that a few blacks were fighting alongside them, and he didn't care what color any one was as long as everyone helped each other stay alive long enough to get home. 'Course that was one of the reason's I loved your father. Not a bone of hatred in his body. Well, back to the letter.

I remember the day I got a letter hand delivered to me after Hattie had passed. When a letter came hand delivered, it usually meant you were being informed that you were now officially a widow. On this occasion, thankfully, the letter reported Emery was injured and his life had been spared due to the bravery of Adam Whittaker, a fellow officer who would be receiving a Purple Heart for his act of bravery. Turned out Emery healed up fine, but his leg still ached from time to time. Never thought much of it really, and then this letter arrived today, all these years later. Apparently the thing Mr. Whittaker had to get off his chest was that he was not the one who should have received the Purple Heart. Turns out he never saved Emery at all, he just took the credit. In fact, another man both saved Emery and carried him five miles to safety. Emery was unconscious and never knew how close he came to death that day. When he woke up, Adam was there to explain things and he lied through his teeth.

He writes;

Emery Foxworthy,
How could you ever forgive an old fool such as me? I'm afraid to meet my maker without confessing my sins. I can't tell you how sorry I am and I'm full of shame. I was in a real jam, old friend.
Remember my saving your life? Well, no one wanted a black man to get all the credit and it seemed to happen so fast. I never saved your life. I was after the fact to say the least. It was a fellow named Tucker Brown, one of the colors. He was a brave fellow Em, not me. He said it didn't matter to him if he got a Purple Heart or not. He owed his brother, Jedidiah, a favor and that is all. He said his brother loved someone and you belonged to her. He said he promised his bother to protect you because of her love. If ever the situation would arise that you

two found each other in the same place, he'd watch over you like a brother. Said his brother would rather die himself, than see that lady loose the man she loved. I never met a man so strong. Saving you was a mission and he took it very serious. He carried you like a rag doll five miles solid, never stopping, till safety.

When he arrived with you over his shoulder, I was standing beside him and the all the fella's looked at me to step up when the doctor asked who was responsible for saving your life. No one wanted to be outshined by a black man and I didn't want to be shunned by the guys... And that's how it happened. As soon as he knew you were going to be o.k., we parted ways so to speak and we'd nod in pass'n and such, but that was all.

So I got to figuring, if I sent you the heart, you could pass it on to his family, since he seemed to know you I thought maybe there's a chance you knew them. I'm heartily ashamed of myself, Em. I hope you can forgive the ravings of an old fool. If I knew who they were, I'd apologize and send the heart to them direct like. God forgive me.
Your old friend,
Adam Whittaker"

And so that was the first thing to be done. We were now the ones on a mission to find Jedidiah's brother's family, and return a Purple Heart. Just imagining a man on this earth capable of loving a woman so much that he asks his own brother to save the life of her husband so she will never be broken hearted!

Of course I bawled like a baby in front of my daughter who was now disappointed in me for not believing in my mother. That also turned out to be the second thing…Have Clara teach me a thing about faith and how easy it is to lose faith in those we love the most, and sometimes it only takes a whispered rumor. It was so easy for me to forget about the love I knew my parents had for each other. I found myself ashamed. Clara could see my pain.

She leaned into me and whispered, "Gramma wants me to whisper that it will be o.k, Crabby Abby! You're not too old to learn a thing or two from your mother and save what you learned somewhere close to your heart. You'll need to remember for later."

"Clara, this is too much."

"I told yah! It's like she's sit'n right here!"
We sat very quietly until we arrived at a place I had only been to once as a small child. Though Momma wrote about it, I had never been as an adult. We immediately went to Tuesdays and made inquiries. That was where we met Ginger Pennyroyal's grand-daughter, Samantha.
She was at least twenty and with a very serious face, asked us from behind a counter, "Can I help you ladies?"
After reading Momma's chapter about Ginger and all the secrets, I thought it might be possible she already knew about us somehow. I thought I'd take a leap of faith and ask, " Hello, I'm Abby, this is Clara. My mother, her grandmother was Olivia Foxworthy. Were you expecting us?"

Samantha looked at us like we were crazy.
"Expecting you?! Not likely. Excuse me a moment?"
She leaned her head in behind a curtain and said in a loud enough voice, "Momma, can you help me please? Olivia Foxworthy's family are here and they were wondering if we might have been expecting them."
"What's that you're going on about?" asked the voice behind the curtain.
"Momma! We got a white nut bar out here, a few sandwiches' short of a picnic basket and it looks like she brought her kid with her!"
Samantha poked her head back out the curtain, turned to us, smiled and said very politely, "My momma will be right here and we'll see if she can help you both," she looked to me with a raised brow and continued, "And

I'm not sure anyone can help you!" Clara busted a gut laughing and I felt so foolish. Still, I thought it had been worth a try.

"Child, did you say Foxworthy?"

"Hello?" I bravely cleared my throat. "Olivia Foxworthy was my mother. We were wandering if we could speak with you a moment. I'm Abby, and this is my daughter, Clara."

"Ginger said this might happen one day, but I was very young then."

"Are you kid'n? I've heard everything now! I apologize. Guess I should'a known my own Momma had the missing sandwiches from your picnic basket." Samantha stated matter of factly.

"Never mind her! Samantha where are your manners, child?" The woman from behind the curtain came to the counter.

“I’m Ginger’s daughter in law, Milly and this is my girl, Sammy, Ginger’s granddaughter.”
“We are on a search for Jedidiah Brown’s sister-in-law.”
“Oh yes, I remember now, the “Big Love.”
“That was real? With real people?” Samantha was amazed and looked to Clara.
“Oh it gets way bigger than that!”
“You look like you’ve come a long way. Let’s take tea then I’ll walk you up to Bethany’s,” Milly kindly offered.
After a much welcomed cup of tea, Milly walked us up past the graveyard where we saw little Tuesday’s stone.
“Did you know my grandmother was buried on a Tuesday?” I said.
“How strange…”Milly answered.
“You know, thanks to Ginger, your

kin are just about famous ‘round these parts. I heard there was a book out. People talk. Is it your Momma’s book?”

“Yes. After she passed, we found some memoirs scattered around the house and one thing she wished she had done was get a book published. She liked mysteries but I think she’d be proud of what my brothers and I have done in her memory.”

“That’s got to be one of the sweetest things to touch my ears. One day I’d like to read that book. Wouldn’t it be something to be in a book? My Lord! Well! Here we are.”

I looked to Clara and winked. If there was enough information, we would definitely make another book for Momma and Milly would be in it.

We approached a turn in the path that we could have never guessed would reveal the most rickety house we had ever seen and on the front veranda sat the most beautiful woman I think I'd ever seen. She sat bare foot in a white rocking chair and she wore a white flowing dress. She had a slight smile on her face that made me realize that's just how her face was, not that she was actually smiling. She was taking in the day and as the sun shone on her face, I saw a slight glow around her from the sun's reflection off her white dress.

Milly noticed my reaction and leaned into me.

"Not to worry, Abby. She's harmless. She's been beautiful ever since God made her. She can't help how she looks. She's just that way. You should see men around her, get all stupid and tongue tied and the likes. You leave the introductions to me."

"Bethany!" Milly shouted in a raised voice.
"Milly! Is that you, Honey?"
"Yeah, and I have a surprise for you like you ain't had in years, my dear!"
"Well, you are all very welcome. C'mon up here then and let's just see who we have here."
"Beth, do you remember Ginger go'n on about the Foxworthy lady?"
"Let's see now. You mean Jed's Big Love, Olivia Baker as once was?"
"That's the one!"
"Oh my Lord, yes. We played together when we were just kids. Sure brings me back a ways."
"This lady here, calls herself Abby and this young one is Clara. They are Olivia's daughter and grand baby."
"My Lord! My Lord! I mean I heard about'm but never thought I'd ever

meet'm in the whole course of my life!" Bethany was excited.
"They have the need to speak with you about your man, Tucker."
"You come all this way to mention Tucker Brown?" Beth's eyes welled and she gently bit her bottom lip, trying not to cry.
"If Olivia was Jed's big love, you got'a know, Tuck was mine."
A moment passed as I stood and looked to Clara. We were like two fish out of water. Clara took the lead.
"Well m'am, if you don't mind much, we have news and something to give you and something to tell you to look for, and lastly a favor to ask, if you don't mind."
"I'm all ears youngster."
"Well, my Gramma Olivia kept an old trunk and she left it to me because I loved it. Anyhow, just lately in fact, I

discovered a secret section, a false bottom."

"This is getting good." Bethany was sincerely interested.

"Well, in it my Gramma Olivia had instructions specifically for me to follow whenever I found the bottom."

"Go on, child. Feels like a mystery beginning to unfold."

"You have no idea."

I shot Clara a look.

"Well, it seems my Grampa Foxworthy was injured in the war and might have died if it weren't for the bravery of a Mr. Tucker Brown, from St. Joseph Missouri."

"My Tucker Brown?"

"The very same, M'am. My Gramma trusted me with the great responsibility of righting a wrong done to him long ago, and return the Purple Heart to the man who did the deed. My Grampa was unconscious the whole time so he never knew Mr. Brown carried him five miles to safety after saving his life in the first place."

"But how is it you know for certain?"

"Well, there's the letter from Mr.Whittaker, who was given the Purple Heart, confessing to my Grampa. Unfortunately, my Grampa passed before him and my Gramma felt the task should lay with me to set things right."

Clara pulled out the Purple Heart and the letter from Whittaker.

"Not here, young one." Bethany rose. She stood, grabbed her shoes and we made our way back down the path, until we stood in front of Tuesday's grave.

"This little grave means the world to me. Do you know your Great

Gramma taught her to read?" Bethany spoke to Clara as though she had the power to bless people, reverence of some kind as though she came from royalty.

"I believe I did hear something about that." I remembered back to Gramma's memoirs.

"Tuesday, mostly because of Ginger, set standards for us who lived around these parts. Had she lived, she could have written letters to your great grandmother. Can you understand what that means?

To know that the world expects you to fail, holds you down, and you have one who holds you so high in her heart that she expects you to be not just her equal but can't imagine life without you when others just like her, never even see you as a human being?"

"No, I can't imagine." Clara was saddened and moved by Bethany's sincerity and was grateful not to know that horrible feeling.

"I wouldn't wish that know'n on anyone. Abby, Tuesday is my second Aunt. A little girl I never knew and she inspired a world of thought in my heart and in my mind. To learn I am who I am was a life-long lesson. I often pass this way and whisper, "Thank you little one. You changed my world."

The way Ginger told it, we around these parts all hold your Momma in our hearts, Abby. I know how it looked and I remember Jed's heartbreak."

"You remember Jed's heart break?" I asked as Bethany nodded and carried on walking.

I wanted to know more but it wasn't the right time. We walked on and when we stopped, we stopped in front of Tucker Brown's gravestone.

Clara leaned down placing the Purple Heart instinctively over the gravestone of its rightful owner.

"Welcome home." I heard Clara whisper.

Beth leaned into Clara and put her hand over her shoulder.

"You are your grandmother's grand baby if ever there was one, right down to that mop head of beautiful curls."

Beth had tears in her eyes. I didn't expect it. I guess I thought pretty people were always insincere. Boy! Did my mother's words come back to haunt me. On the way back, Bethany thanked us.

"Many thanks to you ladies, youngest of ladies included."

Milly had been very quiet during the entire encounter.
"Old friend, are you with us? You look a little concerned as of late."
"Well Beth, I've known you these forty years at least. Guess I'm surprised is all." Milly looked bewildered.
"Well, maybe you should have a seat. Maybe you should all have a seat, 'cause there's more!" Clara instructed.
"Clara? What more? That was it I thought."
"Oh Mom! What am I going to do with you?"
"Clara!" I protested her tone of voice.
"What more could there be?" Bethany was curious.
"As God is my witness, you are all giving me one of my spells!" Milly huffed.

"Clara, if you would just carry on before I pop a gasket over here! I swear! It's like the mystery that never ends!" Milly rubbed her forehead as though she were in pain.

"Well there was another letter that Jedidiah wrote to Gramma."

"Another letter?"

"Clearly this child leads a secret life thanks to my Momma!" I chirped in.

"In it, was instructions for Tucker's wife, Bethany," Clara continued.

"That is it!" Milly raised her hands. "Beth where are the smell'n saults?" And she went into the house. Bethany was about to follow. Clara piped up, "If you please, M'am."

Torn between her friend and the seriousness of moment, Beth shouted, "Milly! First cupboard to the right! Go on, child!"

"Well, I am to read the letter to you instead of you reading it yourself. Not because any one questions your ability to read, but to spare your anger from get'n the best of you."

"Very well." Bethany gave Clara a presumptive slightly irritated look.

It was obvious that Beth's patience were overcome. Obviously someone knew to warn for her anger.

"Ok. So here goes."

I could see Clara was emotional.

"Gramma Olivia wants me to tell you that she remembers you often and hopes you are still beautiful as ever."

I had to sit down at this point as did Bethany, in her chair, she looked like an angel, of course.

"Gramma wants me to tell you she always knew Tucker was very brave and deserving of all good things. Even as children he only had eyes for you and she wants you to know she always hoped you would marry Tucker. My Gramma remembered you very well, obviously, 'cause you are still so beautiful! I thought I would throw that in because I think after all this hard work I wasn't planning on, I can observe for myself, we've clearly got the right Bethany and Tucker here!"

We all laughed. Once again in true Clara fashion, she lightened the mood and carried on. My daughter, I think, became my hero that day.

"So, we move on to the business at hand, a direct message from Gramma Olivia, not me…

"Wish I could there. Bethany, one of my earliest and best friends as a child, besides Jedidiah. Thank Heaven's for Aunt Ruth!

Dear Lord, when I got Whittaker's letter, could'a knocked me over with a breeze! What a small world! Now it's time old friend, to share the "Big Love".

I've sent my granddaughter and I trust she does a great job. She ought to know fine people as you exist in the world still after I have gone. Jed sent me a letter once he had never opened himself. He asked me to keep it till after he was dead and gone and I did that. It was a letter from your beloved Tucker, to you, strangely enough. Hope it holds everything in life you deserve. Having known you, it can only hold good.

Always, Olivia."

"Well, isn't that a fine kettle of fish you have there!" Milly finally

commented through an open window out the veranda.
"I suppose this is Olivia's way of solving mysteries after all!"
"Maybe," Clara answered.
"Are you ready, M'am?"
"To be sure young one," Bethany gripped both arms of the chair in anticipation.
Clara's voice was choppy and this made Beth's eyebrows force themselves together in curiosity, compassion and just a titch of dread.

"Dear Bethany, my Beloved wife...
I have written to Jed and asked him to keep this safe, as it is for you. I love you with all my heart as I am more than sure you have heard millions of times before. You are beautiful to look at to be sure, but you, sweet love of mine, mother to my children and

beloved owner of my heart, you are more than what any set of eyes can see. You are my world. You are what makes me live.

I settled a debt today. I don't need to tell you how, but it's not the first time Olivia Baker as once was, comes into our lives. Seems odd things surround her. Maybe even god walks with her a while from time to time.

Remember when we were kids and I was too shy to even speak with you? There was one day when Olivia was visiting. We were at the swimming hole and you almost drowned? I stood paralyzed with fear and Jed saved you, remember? Well I made a promise that day. I think we were nine years old but still. I promised Jedidiah that I would pay him back because I had Big Love for you in my heart, the kind he said he had for

Olivia. I could swim like a fish Beth, but you in danger, I lost all good sense. I didn't know how or when I'd repay him, but he saved my life when he saved yours. That's when I knew. I knew that day I'd love you for even longer than I drew breath. So I started saving in secret. I saved a penny here and a nickel there and I put in it my tin. On the day we married, I kept my promise a secret and my savings. It was all for you and the kids I prayed we'd have together. I love you more than my own life, Bethany Brown, my wife, my breath. I know we had our moments as married couples do, but I was planning to love you forever since I was nine years old. I knew you'd pick me when we came of age,' cause I could see you, really see you. I knew, my sweet Bethany, and I keep you with me. I love you still. I hope this letter finds you, in case something ever happens to me in this God forsaken war, I wouldn't want you to think I wasn't planning ahead. Imagine a black man planning ahead in this world, in these times. Big Love, that's what it's all about, and I love you forever.

If you are reading this, it's because I'm gone but I'll never be far away, I promise you that.
All my love,
Tucker"

Bethany went into the house and didn't come out for ten minutes solid. She cried like a baby and we could hear. Brothers, romantics and lovers of the women in their lives right to the end. It's no wonder Clara was crying that day when she found the letters and knew what she had to do. She was old enough to understand sacrifice and love, live outside of her fourteen year old world and take it all in…

When Bethany finally returned, she apologized for her tears and took her seat in the rocking chair she was in when we had first met.

"Bethany, there's just a bit more."

"Like what child? I swear I've about had my fill!"

"Look up." Clara directed.

"Look up?" Bethany hesitantly looked up.

"All this to see a smoking tin? Child, I see that tin every day!"

"Says here, you are supposed to look in the smoking tin like it's the first time you have ever seen the thing."

Beth rose and reached for the tin saying while she stretched, "Tuck always took tobacco from the tin after we ate you see, and had himself a smoke. After he passed, I left it there. I miss him, you know how it is. It became like a keepsake and even our kids were not allowed to touch that tobacco tin."

"Well, Gramma Olivia seems to think you should look in it now."

"This has got to be the most bizarre day of my entire life, but I'll look." Bethany sat in the chair, made herself comfortable and opened the tin slowly.

"Well,?! What's in it, a grapefruit?! I swear, I cannot take the suspense! I'm com'n out there Bethany!" Milly's jaw dropped.

There we stood, me, Clara and Milly and Bethany staring at $3000 dollars at least!

Milly flat out fainted, Clara had to sit on the step, taking care of her and I stood dumbfounded.

"All those years, I rocked in this very chair, need'n money, wish'n for the kids and all along, above my head, Tucker had this waiting…"

Bethany rocked, repeating herself time and again. Clara whispered in her ear and Bethany answered, "Of course, child."

I reached into the bag I carried and gave her a copy of The Memoirs of Mrs. Olivia Foxworthy. The book was special. After all, Olivia Brown, Bethany's niece, was mentioned and that would really mean something to Bethany.

We bid our farewells and headed down the path in complete silence.

After a few minutes I had to ask, "Clara, did you know what was in the tin?"
"No, but I know why he didn't tell her himself."
"Why?"
"He thought she'd spend it on the kids and then have nothing to be an old woman on. Turns out she gets it when she's past needing it. He didn't know his kids would be doctors and lawyers."
We laughed and laughed. Seems Tucker needed a lesson much the same as I did about faith in those we love. We hadn't yet seen a photograph of Tucker, but we sure felt like we knew him. A love like that? How could you not know just a little bit about a stranger who loved like that? Guess things were different then. Clara and I had a lot to talk about as

we followed our next set of instructions, including how my mother came into possession of that book. We also had to figure out when was I going to get to read it!

“What did you ask Bethany as we left?”

“If she minded that I needed to keep Jed’s book and a special photograph for a bit ‘cause there’s more to be done.”

“There’s more?”

And in my head I thought, “There you go again Momma! It’s always Olivia! Clearly there was more reading and more to discover.

Chapter Three
The Great Exchange

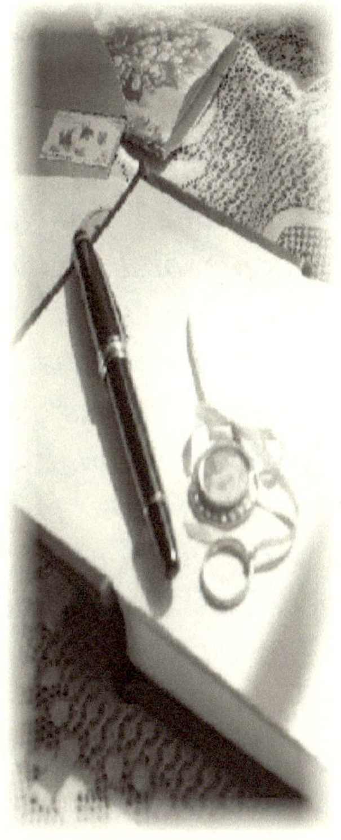

Chapter Three
The Great Exchange

Clara shared our next revelation.
"Dear Clara
I wanted you to read this when I'm gone. Hopefully time has turned you into the young person I always hoped you'd be. Strong, and sensitive, but not stupid! There's never been a stupid Baker that ever was and if that's how you turned out, it came completely to you by your father's side. I just wrote that for your mother's benefit. We always joked. She knows I love the man who loves my only girl alive.
By now, you've found out about Jedidiah and if you followed instructions like I hoped, you've met my childhood friend, Bethany. She's

something! Been that way her whole life.
So, you've been introduced to a thing we called the Big Love back when we were just straps of children. Enclosed is a photo of Tucker Brown with his older brother, Jedidiah. It is very rare and very precious."

I had to take a moment. There we were on the bus, on the way home staring at these two strangers who have changed our lives forever and now we had faces to match. It was like the world transported us into another time so dear and so precious, I could almost smell the sweet grass that held my Momma' s heart in an imaginary Jedidiah and Olivia Country.
Looking at her first love brought a tear to my eye. He was so handsome,

and sweet, and had a smile that went ear to ear boasting the most perfect teeth. Tucker was only a few inches shorter and suddenly something became painfully clear to me. Though she loved my Daddy eternally, she had already been loved and loved in such a way that nothing could touch that place in her heart. That place, and that time belonged to her and Jedidiah and looking at the photo, anyone could see, they owned the moment and deserved the love they knew. I became ashamed I ever thought ill of her. I understood the power of her heart now and the love going around and around, the love that saved my father's life so Jed's love wouldn't be without hers. It was almost too overwhelming. I looked to Clara. "Stop blubber'n Mom! We got work to do. Anyhow, in a letter Gramma wrote to me for my eyes only, she said you and daddy had something the likes of the Big Love and that's how I got here so beautiful!" Clara said smugly boasting even more beauty than she thought she possessed.

Once again, I was thanking my Momma in my mind and in my heart, remembering how she also spoke with her own Momma discovering truths.

"I don't mean to bust your chops, but if that did you in, wait till you read about how she got the letters."

I took one last look at the photograph and I imagined if they had any idea how fine they would turn out- a war veteran who saved my father's life, a teacher, and my Momma somewhere in the midst of all this in a world riddled with prejudice.

"Well, are you ready?"

“Yes. I am still the parent you realize?”
“Yes, M’am, alias Crabby Abby!”
“Alright get on with it.”
Clara handed me the rest of the letter.

“Well, you will have to imagine and it won’t be easy because the world is a very different place now. Back in the day, the streets were very new and just dirt. Nothing fancy like in the big cities, but in our small city, people were always brushing themselves off to show to others they were quality and dirt was beneath them.
On one fine Saturday, I window-shopped with my Momma. Now years had passed since the Aunt Ruth incident when Momma discovered Jedidiah. I was fourteen years old by this time. Momma was babbling about a dress she saw in a shop window and

I was actually ignoring her slightly. That's when I felt the hair on the back of my neck stand straight on end. I got the distinct impression someone was looking at me, hard like. Momma kept babbling away and I turned ever so slightly looking over my shoulder. There he was! A tall black boy was coming right at me. It was like time went in slow motion as Momma kept going on about that confounded dress, I could hear her in the background of my mind, and I stared at that boy. In my heart of hearts I was captured in a trance, I could not break from the sight of him and when he smiled, I knew! It was my Jedidiah! I could hear my heart pound'n! I was overcome. It was like seeing a ghost. My heart came back to me in ways I never knew. He walked in a straight line in my direction and from inside his chest coat, he removed a book and slipped it to me, touched my hand ever so gently, he made my knees buckle, and I slipped that book into my chest coat like we had rehearsed a million times over. My heart leapt! I think I stopped breathing and was that boy fine! He was just how imagined! Strong, intelligent looking, and with that smile!

As he passed by me and I had the book tucked away, he turned and smiled at me again. Momma caught his gaze.

"Now, I told you a million times! If you make eye contact, they'll never leave you alone! Now how about this dress?" She turned and looked back into the window.

I looked back to Jed and he mouthed the words, while walking away backwards, "I love you, always, Olivia Baker."

He bowed and waved like a butler did for a rich person bid'n farewell and I didn't know myself. I couldn't run to him, hold him close and breathe him in. I couldn't cry revealing our secret. Momma would have popped a gasket and that day would have been a different day.

He could see I knew. He could see my heart was his. I mouthed the words, "I love you still, Jedidiah Brown".

He smiled and with a closed fist, he pounded his heart and brought his fist to lips, kissed it gently and blew it over to me. I almost fell over. I placed my two fingers over my mouth and blew a kiss over to him. He grabbed the air like it meant his life, took hold of my kiss and pounded it into his heart, wearing the biggest smile.

Once again, I watched my Jedidiah walk away. Once again my heart was breaking. I thought how cruel God can be and then I thought I'd rather have a world with Jedidiah and the Big Love in it, even if we couldn't be together. A world without him would mean I couldn't exist at all.

When he saw I was about to cry, he mouthed the words, "It's alright." He patted his chest and I remembered the gift he gave and it made me smile back and he nodded back to me with a wink. He knew I loved him still by the look on my face, and that knowing seemed to make him float away that day with happiness.

Momma was still babbling on in the background and when she finally took notice of me, my Jedidiah was gone from my view forever.

"For Heaven's sake child! I swear it looks like you've seen a ghost! Do you have a fever? Something is not right here! Are you well? Truly, you look un- well! Let's get you home to bed!" That's where I did all my digesting of the situation. While I thought as my childhood years passed, he would have moved on with his heart even when I couldn't, it wasn't that way. He had more faith in me than I had in him it seems. No one's fault, really. Friends like Jedidiah don't grow on trees, and the love, the Big Love, is surely a gift from God, maybe the biggest. I thought then, in my fourteen year old world I'd go to him if ever I died. We'd meet in the country we created in our hearts. I figured that's what heaven must be, the happiest place our hearts can find, the place where the Big Love found our hearts

and saved us from all the bad there ever was.

The whole encounter must have lasted but a few moments, yet I remember that day like yesterday.

Every girl should be loved with the Big Love. That's what Jed called it and I know of none bigger, except for the love of mother and child.

I'm telling you this, Clara, because it explains how I got to be in possession of this wonderful gift and helped to make me the woman I am today. Even when I lost faith in myself and was uncertain of decisions to be made, I took faith and comfort in knowing I was taking the high road like I ought'a. I knew for a fact I would not be disappointing my blood brother, my first best friend and first love who believed in me to the very end of time. It's a huge responsibility and one I took very seriously. I've heard a person only lives once, so why not do it the best it can be done?"

Luckily the bus ride home gave two blubbering idiots the time to collect ourselves while completely running out'a hankies! We certainly hadn't planned on the emotional journey we found ourselves on. Seemed like we found ourselves crying every day! There was still more to catch up on reading though and for that we would need to rest. Had I known what was coming,. Never mind, we can't prepare for things. I know that now. I don't know why Momma put a few memoirs in with these papers but they arrived, so they are included.

Chapter Four
Amos & The Missing Letters

Chapter Four
Amos & The Missing Letters

Before I get started, I have to say that God works in mysterious ways, and it may sound repetitive, but I have no other way of accounting for it. Until I met Amos, I never knew him the whole of my life. He came into my life by God's will and left the same way.
I can tell you Amos Cornelius is a man worth mentioning. Amos is a man who believed in the power of the unbelievable, and also he believed there is no such thing as coincidence. What you haven't realized is that Jed filled his book with a sentence to me every day. He carried the book with him just in case he ever saw me. He secretly believed we would meet one day. He prayed for it, believed it, and lived in the notion of it. But in the

event God was busy, Jedidiah thought to send a couple letters my way by post. Must'a taken him months to save up for the postage. Well, I never did receive those letters until, let me see, I was married and Nathaniel was just walking. There were two letters and they somehow were lost in the post. Amos, a young postal worker and believer in the unbelievable miracle of life and wonder, found two crumpled up, old letters in a back room that had fallen behind a cabinet. He opened the letter, and read its contents, realizing the letters were twenty years overdue. He was a romantic and to read Jed's words shamed him.

He set out to find me. He made it his mission like Don Quixote, setting things right in heroic fashion. The letters were very important.

One was the very one you have returned to my old friend Bethany and the other one was a love letter to me.

"Dear Olivia,
Hope this letter finds you well. Life is hard here, Livvy. The flooding of Missouri has taken almost everyone's home and it's a very sad state of affairs. Decided to be a teacher so I am expanding my vocabulary, or trying to anyway. I surely miss you. When you left, loneliness found me and looking back, losing you was worse than the flood. My heart felt more like a rock, heavy and such.
I still don't know when or if I'll ever see your beautiful face again. I write a little something to you and I keep it in my book like a fool, hoping to run into you one day. I write here and there as if I got to see you in passing

like before. I imagine bumping into you and the likes, so I write a greeting sometimes, how are you sometimes and like today, I write I wish you were back with me so my other missing part of my heart was together in the same place.

God knows how I love you, Livvy, and if I pray hard enough and be the best I can be, I'll settle for not even hearing your voice talking. Just a chance to see your pretty face, give you the book and I'll be on my way...Doesn't seem like too much to ask, but in a big world, who knows?

Livvy, sometimes, when I am very quiet, I get to remembering how you would sneak up and bear hug me from behind. You would breathe me in and I can still feel the gentle touch of your nose on the back of my neck, breathing out. I always knew you were coming up to me, but there was no way on God's green earth I would pass up a chance to feel your breath across my neck. Lord, I miss you, girl. I love you always, your Jedidiah."

I sat in the chair when Amos delivered the letter and he asked if I would read it right then and there. Amos told me about his mission and admitted he wasn't certain what this meant to him exactly but he felt certain all would come to light soon. He thanked me and on his way down our walk, he bumped into Rosie, our young neighbor. She was stopping by to bid farewell as she was moving and when she and Amos locked eyeballs, the earth stood still. Amos turned to me and winked. Well, this made me smile. His mission had been revealed. Any other day, any other hour, he would have missed Rosie and they would have never met or maybe God would have found another way to bring them together. Anyhow, they were married shortly after that. No coincidences there!

But what the letter did for me, was make me stronger. To have a received a letter twenty years after it was written, telling me how Jed hoped and prayed for me to get that book, and to have actually received that book never having gotten the letter, proving Jed's unwavering love.

My Goodness! My mind went on in circles. Even your father had to admit that was really something. Of course I told him everything!

Then all those years later, to receive Mr. Whittaker's letter and Tuck's letter also needing to find their way to my old friend Bethany!

And even Amos the believer in the unbelievable, what a part he played. Anybody else might have just thrown away the letters. So you see, if a person doesn't believe in coincidence then in my mind that only leaves God work'n in mysterious ways.
Feels like I'm a rambling old fool some days writing about what I feel is important when you children might find it dribbling.

~Always, Olivia

Chapter Five
Bark'n Dog Chili

Chapter Five
Bark'n Dog Chili

I have to take time to write about your father. Emery Foxworthy was one of the best men I ever knew. I loved him in such a way that every hour, every day I live, I miss the man. I know he's gone and still I whisper little phrases and expressions out loud that I know made him laugh.

When we were first married and I was just learning to cook, I thought I'd surprise him with chili. Now let's see, oh yes, this was just before we moved in with his parents and Hattie hadn't yet arrived.

He loved chili. When he arrived home and the house smelled of it, he was so excited. Because he got whisked away to war, there were not many evenings we had together where I could do this sort of thing and times were tough so we ate a lot of bread, I can tell you that much.

He sat down and took a big mouthful and was about to tell me about his day. We always did that. He always wanted to know how my day was. I always wanted to know how his day was. Some people never asked each other but we loved each other and wanted to know how we each spent our hours apart. We lived our lives like that.

With his first bite of chili, he just stared at me. Then he went white as a sheet. Then he went red as a tomato.

"Em?"

He just smiled in pain like, while perspiration began to pour down his face.

"W...wwh..." he couldn't manage to get the word out.

"Em, what in heaven's name?"
He stood up and began prit' near choking. He ran to the sink and got himself a drink of water, then another one and then another. By the time he was able to speak, his voice was raspy and his throat was in pain.
"Olivia, my love, how much of the chili powder did you use?"
"Just a titch. I know how you love eat'n chili, Em, so I thought I'd jazz it up a little."
He closed his eyes and swallowed hard. "Jazz it up?"
He looked to the counter and saw the paper bag of spice I had saved up to buy as a surprise. He picked it up and read the label.
Still coughing and with tear filled eyes he asked, "Olivia does this bag read right?"

"Yes, it certainly does! Cayenne pepper for my sweetheart of a man!"
"And was this a full bag at one time, dearest?"
"Yup! What a good idea I had. Aren't you surprised?"
"Oh, I'm surprised alright. How much would you say you used?"
"Oh, just a titch."
I began to get worried over this line of questioning.
"Olivia I thought you said this was a full bag."
"Yes," I answered.
"What in heaven's name is a titch exactly?"
"It's one of these."
I took a healthy pinch and tossed it in the sink.
"Oh my sweet Olivia. We haven't been married long I know, but I think I got this one figured out."

"My recipe is supposed to be a secret, Em. The trick is to use a titch here and there at the top of the hour and really cook it good, all day like."

"Heaven knows I love yah, but I promise I can't barely swallow the stuff. You did a bit too good on the spice I think."

"Oh, I see." My heart sank and when he saw how disappointed I was not to be able to give him a good dinner, in true Emery fashion, he came over to me and held me.

"Now, now, Olivia. Don't you worry your pretty head about it. Truthfully, I was hoping for leftover meatloaf."

My spirits lifted and we laughed at the whole just a titch thing.

"Now I don't mean to hurt your feelings any but if you don't mind I have a favor to ask. There's this one fellow at work, the complaining type.

Always borrowing tools in the shop and never returning them, tak'n bites of fella's lunches before they get to break, you know the likes."

"Sounds to me someone needs to have just a titch of my extra special chili!"

"I like how you think!" Em was now able to swallow.

"Also the barking dog down the way probably needs a titch as well!"

"Done, my dear!" We giggled.

When Em came home the following night he was giddy with excitement.

"Livvy ! You'll never guess, so I'll just tell yah. Ike went in ahead of everyone today and sniffed out the chili, and took well, more than a titch! His face went red as a tomato! Me and the guys thought he stopped breathing and then he smiled and laughed out loud! I mean he laughed out loud! Some guys have been there

for ten years and never heard a chuckle from the guy and there he was, laughing out loud! Turns out, it tastes just like his Momma used to make and he loves the stuff. We all got to know him today and I swear, there's something about you. God finds a way to work through you and I married yah! You know what that makes me?"

"What?" I asked even though I confess I was nervous about what the answer would be.

"Either the poorest damn fool of a fella whoever did live or the luckiest man on God's green earth just because you love me. I'm stick'n with blessed. I love you, Livvy."

Momma's account of my Father was so life-like, I found I hadn't finished bawling on that fool bus after all.

Chapter Six
Hattie In Our Eyes

Chapter Six
Hattie In Our Eyes

And that's what it was like between me and your father. Enough about food! Guess food was just so scarce, life and survival revolved around it. I'd like to tell you about a side of Emery you never knew. We didn't know each other long before we married. It wasn't romantic at the very first. The world was in turmoil and sure, we cared, even loved each other but it wasn't until we married there came what I call "the knowing". Things were different then, not like now where people get up to all sorts of things before they get married. You can imagine the jitters on the wedding day!

A promise like that was the biggest thing in the world and it meant forever to most of my generation. Life was different, serious, loyal and for all the uncertainty in the world, that promise was something to be relied upon, valued, treasured, never lied to, something worth living for, and something worth dying for. It may seem from past writings that I gave the impression getting over Hattie and her passing and that whole time of our lives was my own doing...well it wasn't. Emery's passion, his very make-up, his heart and soul kept us in one piece the whole of our lives. Your father was strong and true. Oh, my Lord! The man was good, through and through, smart too, real sharp like. Back in the day, he was fine. He was pretty tall, very strong, broad shoulders, strong arms, heavy set and not skinny. Never found too much to look at the skinny kind, but that's just me. Guess kids today say handsome and such the likes. I still think God sent him to me. I can't imagine not ever having know'n him. He's my very best friend in the whole of the world. I only hope that all my children marry their best friend. It can keep a person strong. There's nothing like the love of your best friend, someone who knows the very heart of you when life tests you with joy and sadness, disappointment and heartache. It's a quiet understanding and a knowing and an acceptance...

Oh yah, back to the knowing...well my wedding night was how shall we say-eventful to say the least. No gutter talking now!

There was no such thing as going away to far and exotic places. We rented a one room cottage and it felt like we were royalty. The local grocer gave us a cheap bottle of wine and cheese in a basket and an Italian loaf of bread and that was our feast!
We were so happy to be with each other that night and as the night moved on, and the bottle emptied, we lay in each other's arms just staring into each other's eyes. When that man held me close I felt certain nothing bad could happen to me, or even touch me. We stared into each other's eyes before, but not like this. At that moment, in the candle light, it felt to me like I had leapt clear into his heart and that was exactly where he wanted me. So emotional and honest in the silence I think we knew then we'd truly love each other forever. He

really knew he could trust me and he actually could feel my love intensely. And that was exactly how I wanted him to feel- loved by me. We really would have died for each other and from what I understand from my quilting evenings, not every woman felt that way about their husbands. Of course I realize as young newlyweds we didn't know what we were get'n into but we knew we'd rather be together than apart ever again.

Later that night, it began raining harder than it had been raining the rest of day. Did I mention what a rainy day my wedding day was? The gentleman who rented the cottage to us said that if the roof was to leak, to just put a kitchen pot under the drip and he'd take care of it in the morn'n.

Well, must'a been the middle of the night when we heard a tremendous creaking sound. The rain had already stopped but the roof had surely collected a lot of rain.
"What was that?" I asked Em.
He said he wasn't sure but we might be need'n that pot the gentleman mentioned earlier and asked me to get it.
I opened the blanket and covered up again. It was cold.
"Sorry, Livvy. I didn't realize it was so cold."
He got up to fetch the pot as the roof began leak'n a bit heavy.
"Damn! It's so cold and dark I can't find noth'n. Oh, alright now, I think I found it."
And at that exact moment, as Em turned back towards the bed, the tremendous creak'n sound turned into

a huge gushing, crashing and swooshing sound.
There your father stood at attention, butt naked in the middle of the room completely drenched, in the moonlight, as the roof had given way, still holding that fool pot up to catch the drips. He stood in shock as not even a piece of wood or shingle had fallen on him, only around him.
"Em? You alright?"
"Yah- I'm think'n I could'a used a bigger pot!"
"Livvy?"
"Yes, Em?"
"Are you laugh'n over there in that warm dry bed fully know'n this could'a been you if I wasn't a gentleman?"
"Yup!"

"Evil woman! When I dry off I'm gonna make those sheets warm again!"

Oh my goodness we laughed that night! One of the best times we ever had, course there were so many, but that one was definitely one of the best. When two people are lucky enough to find that adult love to have for their lives, it's a gift, an irreplaceable friendship. I was fortunate to love as a child and even more fortunate to love and be loved as a woman.

I still remember when I told your father about Hattie being on the way and such. What a moment. All these moments add up in a person's quality of their life, you know. All the loving really matters, every day like, and not just on anniversaries.

Your father got down on his knees and pulled me close.

"Thank you, Livvy. You growing my child, our child, the child we made. God knows I love you!"

He had a tear in his eye and finally one fell, which made me cry- in part 'cause I was the woman and didn't cry first, but mostly because he made me realize the true miracle and the beauty of it all, even more than I knew.

At that moment, I felt magical almost, something beautiful and special, honored and valued.

Your father didn't walk around the world blubber'n all the time but he cried every time he found out there was one on the way and cried even harder at the moment each one of you arrived. You probably didn't know he was heartbroken not to come in the room for each one of you. He wasn't the type to wait in the waiting room with a cigar. No Sir! He was glued to the door of the delivery room praying for me and waiting for that first baby cry. Corrine from Church used to tell me I married the most sentimental big hearted, manly man there ever was. I was just always feeling complete when he shared his pains and trusted me, knowing how I cared for him. He was firm with you kids but never out of hand.

Your father and I had very similar colored eyes. Just a fact, but his eyes were so beautiful to me, and he wasn't vain, but he would admit he also liked the color of his eyes, hazel green-brown and they always were changing. He would tell me he loved the color of my eyes and I'd answer that he should like'm 'cause they're prit'near the same as his. His response to that with a chuckle was that he never passed a mirror he didn't like.

I always figured he could speak with his eyes. Sometimes when we were together, we liked to sit in the silence of each other. I could hear him breathing and I'd look into his eyes and he'd give me that brat smile of his and we never had to speak. We just knew. There are no words to use that would be appropriate for a moment like that. It's just a know'n, a know'n and a belong'n.

Ever since our wedding night, he looked at me that way and every night after that. He was so beautiful to me, just like I thought a man should look and be.

One last thing is the trust. We loved each other in such a way that nothing or nobody could separate us. Even if we hadn't spoken and a situation

appeared that one of us was up to something, it never gave us a moment of concern or suspicion. We knew if everything was crumbl'n around us, we had each other to trust and rely on. No secrets. God knows how I miss the man.
There is just so much to miss some days, but I pray we'll hold each other again one day, God will'n.

When you all were youngsters, your father got to thinking, which is something he did a lot of. Seemed he kept all concerns pretty much rolling around in his head, always thinking about the future, the past, our family. One day he and I drove out to Jedidiah and Olivia country and we placed a beautiful shaped stone at the foot of that tree. In honor of Hattie, never to be forgotten, we buried a few

items we held dear, a time capsule, I guess you could say. He told me he wanted the rock to rest somewhere I valued and treasured and to be part of him. He etched his message on the rock and I'll save that for another time. We neither of us ever forgot and we carried that little one with us each and every day. When my own mother passed, my heart had a clear understanding and I felt her no longer physically near. But with your sister, maybe because she was just a baby when we lost her, she always felt near and sometimes for no reason, the thought of her would pop into our heads like we expected her to enter the room any minute. We just loved so completely, I guess we can't find the words to explain our actions.
He cried that day to be sure, but in his eyes, I could see myself crying and we

held each other crying for a very long while. He said if he looked real close into my eyes, he could see himself and always felt that is where Hattie truly was, between us, within our reflections, our images, your father's bratty smile, his chin, my shape of eyes and my hair, nestled within us and our love forever, Hattie in our eyes.

Chapter Seven
To Walk With Angels

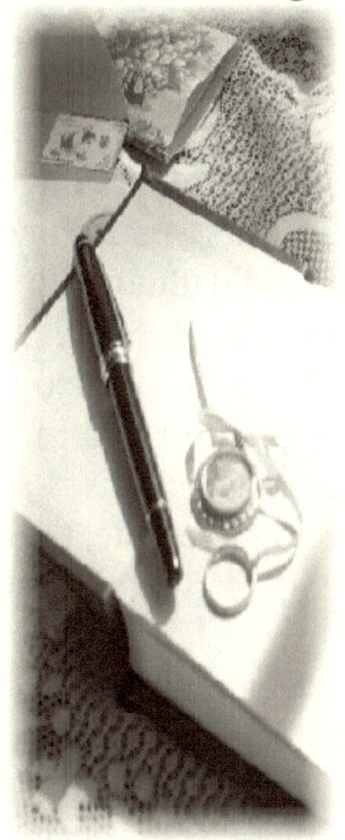

Chapter Seven
To Walk With Angels

This is one of the most difficult things I have ever had to write. After years of discovering memoirs, travelling, setting things right, carrying out deeds to the letter and without fail, this particular task is the "One!"

Other things have happened in the past and my brothers and I found it truly miraculous, but this is so big, so wonderful, so incredible, the only way to describe it is to write it just as it happened.

Clara and I were exhausted having found Momma's Instructions, meeting Bethany, discovering Jedidiah's photo, and there was so much to think about.

Still, we were on what I believed to be a fool's errand. We were to ride the

bus into the city and locate a woman named, Mrs. Elizabeth Caveney. We didn't know yet how this meeting would affect our lives, all our lives. Momma had specific instructions that Clara and I were to go on our own. Clara was to walk up to the door, not me, and ask for Mrs. Elizabeth Caveney. Should Mrs. Caveney answer, Clara was to ask for a few moments of her time and in the event Mrs.Caveney was in fact the correct woman we were meant to see, we were to give her the package Momma had carefully wrapped. We, none of us knew what was in the package. As we approached, Clara turned to me, "Do you think we get to deliver more money?"
"At this point, noth'n Momma has in store for us would surprise me!"

Clara slowly walked up to the door and knocked. She turned to me curiously while I waited back on the sidewalk and I shrugged my shoulders. Suddenly the door swung open and my jaw dropped. Clara looked back to me with eyes as large as saucers!

The lady didn't know what to make of it. She looked to the baby resting on her hip and then at Clara and then at the baby. No one could speak and then suddenly Clara slapped her lap and let loose, "The Laugh."

Then Mrs. Caveney let out a laugh and the two sounded identical. The eyes, the hair, the laugh and the baby! Then they looked to me.

"Oh my God! It's Sweetest of Angels?! I just know it!" I said out loud.

It was lights out for me right there on the street! I flat out fainted in all my confusion and I did it to the nervous laughter of my oldest sister Hattie and my daughter Clara!

Hattie had been found!

“Oh don’t mind Momma. She does that sort of thing quite a bit lately, blubber’n too ,” Clara offered an unflattering explanation.

“We keep her anyhow on account that we love her and such.”

The two laughed as they revived me and we gathered ourselves into the house.

Elizabeth started to cry with joy, and I couldn’t restrain myself. I started to cry also, but that can’t be a surprise to anyone. Clara leaned in and asked, “So! You must be the famous Hattie-Sweetest of Angels?”

"I beg your pardon?" Mrs. Caveney smiled.

We explained about Momma's book, and we gave her a copy. At that point her little baby girl, Emmie played on the floor and a second child came into the room just having woken up from a nap.

"Momma?"

Elizabeth rose and asked her little son, Oliver, if he had a good sleep.

"I swear, this is too much. I think I'm getting a fever. Your children,.. where did you come up with those names?" I asked in a chopped breath.

"My father was in the army with a good man, and a great friend he had lost touch with. He asked me if I ever had children to name them after this fellow and his wife, Emery and Olivia."

"What was your father's name?" I asked fully knowing I just might faint. "Whittaker, Adam Whittaker," Elizabeth said proudly. In my defense, I must announce, I did not faint. "Boy, have we got a lot to catch up on!" Clara beamed with joy at discovering her younger cousins. Elizabeth carried on.

"My parents were great people. They would have loved to have had grandchildren. Unfortunately my father died a few years back and the following year my mother passed away. I had my two a little late in life I suppose. Being an only child, I took care of my parents and time passed. On my mother's death bed she revealed a tale so wild and strange I couldn't believe it was true. After she passed and things settled, I

remembered her words and decided to find out more if possible.
My mother said with tear filled eyes that she and my father were not able to have their own children. That fact devastated my mother. Soon after they were married, my father went to war and since he came from a fair amount of money, my mother who didn't have to work, stayed in a little house across from a neighborhood of row housing in the heart of the city. Well, one day there was a devastating fire. It went through the old houses like match sticks and everyone was in a panic. Just as the fire broke out, the milk man, Elmer, who had become quite familiar with the families who lived there, rushed in from house to house as fast as he could. When he came to the house where I lived, and I was just a baby, he could see that the

older couple in the house had succumbed to smoke inhalation. He noticed me completely wrapped in my blanket and when he nudged me, he heard a noise. He threw off the blanket I had been covered in, handed the baby to a line-up of rescuers, my mother being one, and the words were passed down the line, "The baby's face was covered in a blanket, I think she's fine but her family's gone now . Another orphan made today. Never saw anyone else here but the baby and the grandparents."

My mother felt God put her there that day so in the face of tragedy, she would love that orphan and felt surely that God blessed her that day. Elmer passed away that day saving people. So many people perished and who ever remained found themselves displaced. So she kept me. The only thing I came with was a little sweater with a hand stitched repair that had been done with what looks like an old blanket. You know, I always looked so different from everyone in my family. I always had a feeling, a longing, and I could never explain it." Elizabeth paused, went to a cabinet and pulled out a tiny knitted sweater with a tiny repair on the corner that was made out of a blanket.

"When I began my inquiries, the only name anyone could remember was Foxworthy and there was mention of a baby who died in a fire. I didn't know where to begin and so much time had passed. The Foxworthy's were a small family and so I sent out letters of inquiry. As time passed I received no response.

I figured the Foxworthy's didn't want to know me. I was raised well and had a great life so I bore no real regrets but secretly I hoped someone would find me. Then one day I received a letter from a Foxworthy cousin. Her name is Doris," Elizabeth paused.

"Yes, she and my mother were quite close especially near the end of my mother's life. She was a second cousin to my father. She died even before my mother but within months," I added.

We then supposed she must have told Momma but the two women were so ill, that time did not permit them to investigate fully before informing the rest of us.

I still did not faint.

"I wondered what happened when I didn't hear back. I just figured my life was saved back then, and that would have to be enough. Then my prayers were answered.

I received a letter a few years ago, from a Mrs. Olivia Foxworthy and in that letter I was informed not to give up faith. That she was my mother, that she loved me and was sending someone who would make everything right, now that God had answered her prayers that the impossible could be true. That was years ago and no one came, until now.

Clara looked over to me as I clutched the package completely entranced with every word Hattie spoke. I leaned into to her and handed the package to her. She gently un-wrapped it and sure enough the blanket told the story. In the corner of that blanket was a missing piece that matched perfectly with the little sweater. I could imagine Momma

holding the blanket on that fateful day, realizing her little one had passed and could see her in my mind, sitting devastated on the sidewalk by herself, running her finger over the stitching on the blanket while in her new found pain, looking up to the heavens.
Alright, I know you're all waiting for the words, yah I fainted!
When we finished remembering what must have happened we decided that Momma had fully expected to live long enough to see Hattie. Even though God had another plan for her, she found the strength to have put these items together for Clara to do her task, even as a child, of course knowing the task would fall to me.
Momma was stubborn to be sure and this was most likely the last thing she did before she died, wrote her final two letters.

Now that Hattie was a mother herself, she was returned to her family when she needed family the most, and in doing so, filled a void she now knew she was heartily never prepared to leave behind. Momma couldn't guess that the house wouldn't get sold after her funeral and if that had happened, items would have been dealt with a great deal sooner than when Clara discovered the false bottomed trunk. Guess it's like Momma always said about truths being like small potatoes trying to find the light and eventually they always do. All things in good time…

Clara and I sat silently. We were dumb founded. Then Clara looked over to little Oliver and he asked, "Why do you look like Emmie?" Clara smiled.

"I think you might be o.k. but that one over there is always faint'n and blubber'n. I don't suppose she knows how to have any fun at all!" he said in a sad voice on my behalf, with deep concern in his eyes.

Where do we begin explaining to a four year old?

We laughed and laughed, and we shed a few more tears and we prepared to made our way back home. Before we left Elizabeth's house, Clara said there was one final thing to be done and it included all of us, and when I say all of us, I mean everyone!

It felt like a journey in epic proportions as the Foxworthy clan travelled to Jedidiah and Olivia Country once again, this time all of us four together. With all our children, we stood silent as Elizabeth (Hattie) took her turn following directions

from a mother she never knew but always felt. It was her turn now to be touched by the will of Momma and Daddy as God worked through them at the foot of a tree that touched all our hearts. That tree bound Jed's family to ours, our family to the Whittaker's and the Whittaker's back to Jed's family. What are the odds? Elizabeth ran her fingers over the carving of the heart that Jedidiah had made for Momma. Clara returned the photo of Jedidiah and Tucker to Bethany who stood just shaking her head in wonderment and gratitude with that beautiful face of hers.
"I see little one. Your Gramma needed her lost baby to see Jedidiah for herself so she could really be part of this," Bethany whispered in a chopped breath.

Sammy and Milly stood quietly until Sammy leaned over to Clara and whispered, "Yup, this day is pretty wonderful but I still think y'all are a lot strange!"

She looked over to me and then whispered to Clara again, "Her most of all!" And the two girls giggled like when you're not supposed to laugh while in church.

Bethany breathed in deeply.

"Have you ever seen a day as fine as this?" Bethany asked Clara.

"No m'am," answered Clara as they held hands.

And truth be told as we all gathered there, the sun was setting slowly and just a little bit of fog seemed to start up above the tall sweet grass, gently caressing our view of rolling hills.

Elizabeth knelt and read the rock our father had engraved so many years before. I couldn't believe I had walked that way and never read the rock before, never thought to look for words, never thought to take a moment at Momma's special tree, even if only to take in the view. I sure paid attention now. I sure saw the world differently now…

With tears of joy flowing slowly down her cheek, she moved a large curl of hair away from her face and began to read her father's words aloud.

"I could see forever through your eyes, little one. When those I love remember me when I am gone, they will remember how I love you still."

There wasn't a dry eye amongst us. Life has ways of throwing us and those we love surprises. Momma used to say she thought it was strange that when bad surprises happened, people would swear that God had abandoned them. She would tell us to pay attention at that moment because it's when bad things happen that God is right around every corner to help us along, walk us through it.

As I looked around at the scenery, at my brother's, their wives and children and now our eldest sister returned with her husband and children, finding something so special under a tree that belonged to a country imagined by two kids who for every social reason at the time should have never known each other- all I could do was thank God, and all the powers that be, that Momma and Daddy's faith never wavered, not even once. For even though every sign and indication pointed to the death of Hattie, the fireman at the time told

Momma no one survived, and even when she and daddy both felt the loss of Hattie so profoundly, they couldn't acknowledge her absence in their hearts. They just had a "feeling" and a prayer, and look what happened all these years later?

Momma died knowing Hattie lived and lived well. She died knowing, God for whatever reason, deprived her of Hattie, but could thank God for finding Hattie that day, and keeping Hattie safe and well and loved.

For some, that would have been the driving force behind not believing in God, but for Momma, it just made her faith stronger. She really didn't have any regrets, no unfinished business, but I think this day would have made her heart sore.

Elizabeth's husband took a small shovel and slowly moved the earth from beneath the rock. He placed one hand over Elizabeth's shoulder as she removed a small tin chest. We circled round as she pulled out a wooden rocking horse baby toy Daddy had carved for Hattie, and a little hat and sweater Momma had been knitting. She had it with her while at work sometimes sneaking in a row or two. There was a little pair of brand new shoes, some lavender water baby bath, a photograph of Momma and Daddy, and of course a letter :

"Sweetest of Angels,
My darling girl, in this box you'll find a tribute to our love for you. Two fools we might be, but we are two fools who simply can't live without you. So my dear, we've decided not to.

In the event our prayers get answered and we meet again, we've set aside a few things for you to cherish acknowledging our short time together. Your Daddy carved that toy with his own hands during the war just for you, baby girl. I was sneak'n time during work to knit you a sweater because the one you wore had a mended tare. Can't imagine you going to heaven in that tattered old thing! I am very sorry I knit so slowly. I included a photo so you know what we look like. You have my eyes and floppy mop head of curls and your daddy's chin and his bratty smile to be sure. You laugh like me I think, right from your toes, a big genuine laugh.

We'd been saving up to buy you a pair of shoes and a while back now the store called to give them to us as a keepsake, so we put those in too. Never seen a man so happy as your father as when he held you in his arms. Truly, you brought a joy to us like no other. Your arrival made our lives, our love complete. It's the strangest thing when a person gets news like this and we refuse it in our hearts to be real. You will live forever and a day in our hearts and in our minds. We will never say goodbye to you just because you left first before us. Our hearts wouldn't allow it. So in the very unlikely event that you ever find this small token of our love you will know that God works in mysterious ways, laugh as often as you can, smile for noth'n, love and be loved all your whole life. When and where we walk, you walk with us, now

and forever through this life and the next.
Love Momma and Daddy, Always"

It was Clara who took Oliver's hand and led him closer to his mother who sat on her knees on the grass holding the box. He reached in and took out the rocking horse.
"Clara, what is it?" he asked.
"Oliver, it's a rock'n horse. Grampa Emery made this for your Momma," Clara answered.
Oliver examined the horse very carefully and then leaned in across his Momma, noticing Elizabeth was crying. He plunked himself down on her lap facing her. He was very concerned and wiped a tear from her face.

"Momma? Do you like the rock'n horse Grampa Emery made for yah?" he asked very concerned.
"Yes Oliver, very much so."
"It'll be our secret, o.k. Momma?" The boy offered in his most sincere voice.
"What's that about a secret?"
He held her face in his hands and promised the promise of a lifetime when you are a person with the accumulated wisdom of just about five whole years.
He leaned in, turned her face and whispered in her ear loudly enough for everyone to hear, "It'll be our little secret 'cause you like it so much but I gotta tell ya… Momma that ain't no Rock'n horse," he pulled away from her face with huge sorry eyes and dread to be the bearer of bad news as

he relieved his mother of any doubt in her mind about the gift.

"It isn't?" Elizabeth asked.

For the second time, he turned her head and whispered in her ear.

"No Ma'm! That there thing is made of wood!"

Elizabeth pressed her lips together trying not to laugh at Oliver's sincerity having unearthed a mystery that clearly the entire new family had missed.

"Yes, Oliver. I understand. At this time it would be best to keep it a secret, especially since I like it so much. Pinkie swear?"

"Pinkie swear!" The very proud youngster ran off with his mission of secrecy in tow.

When I saw the two pinkie swear, I imagined two little children still running through the sweet grass, their

voices echoing across time giggling, making dreams for their future, laying side by each, staring up at the very clouds I looked up at now. With every breath I wondered just how this life falls into place every day.
All of this from two small children and a fork in the road that was only that way in appearances. Whichever road one chose to travel, if you travelled that road long enough, it would meet up again, and here we all are today.
Clara looked to me.
She held up a tiny pink folded paper square tied with a piece of twine.
"Last one, momma," she smiled kindly. "Are you ready?"
She wrapped her arm around my waist and we walked away from the family over to the quiet of an old fence. I became consumed with the

idea that fence had been built with love and was very new once. But as the sun set and it cast a shadow, the idea struck me that the fence was old and beautiful still. Paint chipped, wood fallen, even rickety, but still standing, still beautiful.

"It's been quite a journey, Clara. I'm very proud of you."

"Thanks. I did a lot of growing up lately." Clara looked sad as she peered across the gently blowing wheat grass. I moved a floppy curl from across her face and placed it behind her ear.

"What is it, honey?"

"This growing up thing is exhausting!" she admitted half- joking with tear filled eyes.

"I miss Gramma Olivia. I'm just worried that once we open this, it'll really be over." Clara became

overcome with emotion as tears welled up in her eyes.
"Would you like me to share this with you?"
Clara dried her eyes and we sat together in the gentle breeze. We could hear the wind through the leaves of the trees that seemed to sway almost musically in harmony with the grass over the rolling hills.
I slowly untied the twine and together, our hearts knew this little pink paper was the last thing Momma ever wrote to us.
The paper was brittle with age, and I very carefully unfolded it. A tiny plain gold ring fell to the ground. It was the ring my father had given to my mother when he went to war before they were married. Many of the soldiers gave these rings to their wives and girlfriends because it was

all anyone could afford. Inside the inscription read, “Forget Me Not”. I’d never seen my mother without it. A tiny ribbon tied to the ring read, “For Clara.” Clara put the ring on and it fit perfectly. She would wear that ring forever, like a token of honor and all that is good. Every minute of every day, she would feel valued, protected and most of all, that her beloved grandmother and now dear friend, was always with her.

My mother’s words touched us very deeply. Perhaps it was the knowing we would never read any more she had written, but the moment was ours, forever etched in a timeless thought captured in our hearts.

"Dear Abby and Clara,
When I am gone from all sight and sound,
Remember how love keeps go'n round and round.
Please love each other wild and true
And love my Angel,
God returned to you.
Live and love and laugh and smile
And I will walk with you a while.
When you wish I could be near,
Whisper softly and I will hear.
My love will never be far and away
I love you forever and a day.
Always, Olivia."

Of course we cried like babies! Once again, Momma answered a question in need of answering. Clara wondered if the journey was over and if it wasn't, how long would it last.

Set against the wheat field back drop, I knew that moment would bind Clara and I together more than anything else during this whole journey we had shared.

The answer was simple. The answer was in front of us all along. In true Momma fashion she ended every letter she ever wrote with the answer. When does life's journey end? It doesn't! It keeps right on going. The journey lives on in our hearts so the love keeps go'n round and round, happening before us and happening long after we are gone. That's the reason Momma took such great care in living as best she could, loving as strong as she does, knowing one day she would be away from our sight, but never very far away.

I took Momma's advice and whispered across the wheat grass, "Thank you, Momma."

I heard Clara with a tear filled whisper, "Thank you, Gramma Olivia."

We believe she heard us.

And just in case you need to hear it, and when you get to wondering just how long does the journey last, the answer is, "Always".

Chapter Eight
Olivia's Nana Gray

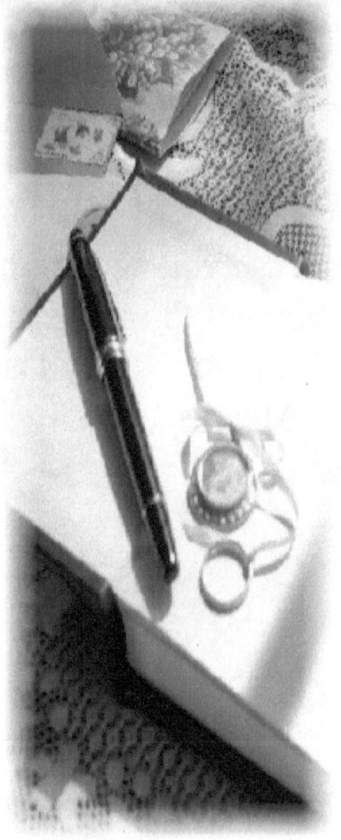

It wouldn't be for four more years until the time came when, just like Momma always said, "Truth will find the light, just like small potatoes and big things come from small potatoes!", that we discovered a memoir about Momma's Nana Gray hidden in the most unlikely of places, in plain sight so to speak. We found it stuffed in a book that sat for years unnoticed on the book shelf, right beside our encyclopedia's. Boy! Were we surprised!

"*Nanna Gray &*
My Inside- Outside- Face

When we are young, we see more clearly than any other time in our lives. Everything that happens is so certainly the worst, the best, the scariest, or the most-ever. All of those first experiences can help shape us or can help hurt us.

Nanna Gray had a way about her, plain and simple. She once told me she got her name because she had a patch of gray hair when she was born, right in the front, about the size of thumb, and it stayed with her the whole of her life. To say I loved Nanna Gray doesn't come close to the gratitude and appreciation I feel as an adult. Also, I miss her and love her dearly to this very day.

Gray came to love and care for me when I was just a child. If ever there was child who needed a grandmother and a woman who needed a grand baby, it was Gray and myself. That's how Gray became Nanna Gray. She helped me make it through when I was so devastated, broken-hearted over Jedidiah and I don't know what would have happened without her intervention, divine it may have been, if you dare to believe in such things.

Back then, we had a double seater swing in the front of our house on the veranda and me and Nanna Gray passed many hours there figure'n, that's what we called it anyhow.

"Nanna Gray? Momma says your kind don't go to our heaven, and I've been figure'n."

"Uh, huh?" Nanna Gray always said that during our figure'n talks.

"Well, I'd like to know if you and I will meet again someday up in heaven and since you are so old, I expect you will get there first."

"Uh, huh , I see!" Nanna Gray raised one eyebrow.

"Not like I'd be wanting to rush anything along 'cause I reckon you are not THAT old."

"Suppose we stop talking about my oldness now maybe, and get onto the figure'n part?" Nanna smiled and pulled me closer. We both sat back and looked out into the sky as we swung in that chair.

"Well, it makes me sad, what Momma said, and I can't imagine God being so bored, he made two heavens."

"I reckon you're right, child."

Nanna saw a bit of a tear in my eye.

"Now don't you be wearing your inside-outside –face another minute, young one."

Nanna Gray always said my outside face gave away what my insides were feeling.

"Well, you know when we went to Old Johnny Post's funeral?"

"Uh, hun,."

"I saw the outside of him go right into the ground!"

"That's right," Nanna wondered what I was thinking.

"Well he was one of you, Momma says."

"I guess, if that's how you see things."

"Then we went to Miss Lucy's funeral and according to Momma, Miss Lucy, well, she was one of us, and her outside went right into the ground. I was really watch'n hard like, Nanna. I saw the whole thing!"

"That's about the size of it. Olivia, that's just how things get done."

"Well, I did me some figure'n and I think I'm really onto something!"

"Uh, huh.." Nanna seemed intrigued.

"Nanna Gray, if we are all of us down here put'n everybody's outsides into the ground, what gets to go to anyone's heaven? I figure, only everybody's insides get to go to heaven, so how do you suppose God sends your folk one way and my folk another way? If there's no outsides to be seen, how does God know what's what and who's who? What the heck is going on up there in anybody's heaven?"

"My, my, you have been doing a lot of figure'n. Maybe only what is on the

inside matters to God, Sweet Pea, and maybe that's why what's inside a person matters so very much in this world and the next."

"I figure you and me are right about this and I reckon there are a lot of people surprised when their insides make it up to heaven and see what's really going on when they have no outsides to think about!"

We laughed and laughed.

"I best be pretty good inside the whole of my life, Nanna Gray."

"That's a very good idea."

"Also, I was figure'n.."

"My Lord! There's more?"

"Well, I was figure'n you're so old, you had a lot of years to get your insides in order, but if I kick it tomorrow, and I get the chance to go first, I'm a little worried my insides are not good as they should be to get into heaven, so how will I get there to be waiting for you? Surely that's where you'll be going, where me and Jedidiah will be going and Aunt Ruth and,.. and I want to be with all of you."

Nanna Gray held me as we stared out into the sky.

"Child, you got the best insides strong and true. We'll see each other again one day. You ain't got noth'n to worry about as long as you fill your insides

up with good every day. You got that?"

"Yes, M'am. Does filling up with good food count? I declare all this figure'n is giving me an appetite, Nanna Gray."

"Child, I cannot keep up with yah. You are a grow'n concern. God knows I love you."

I really liked it when Nanna Gray said that because she would always hug me right after. Hope she has a great big swing chair waiting for me and her up in heaven and also I hope there is plenty of blue sky to help us with all our figure'n.

I once asked after Nana Gray's family, but she never spoke of them. Maybe one day, when I am older I'll find out more and she will let me see what she's always writing in that book of hers."

Mrs. Olivia Foxworthy, this May 13, 1944

Now, you have to wonder just how many lives my Momma actually lived! We had never heard Momma speak of Nanna Gray and it was confusing. I mean, one could suppose the name may have popped up before now.

Flipping through the book, we found more of Momma's memoirs pressed in pages on purpose, creating a timeline, and when we read the words on the pages in that book, we realised the book had belonged to Olivia's Nanna Gray.

Well, seems just as good a title as any for a third book, I suppose, but already there's a different feeling surrounding the start of this adventure. Guess we'll find out why this book wasn't in the trunk.

"Thank you yet again, Momma. Abby, Hattie, Nathan and Jonas and all our children. We love you, Always."

Author Notes

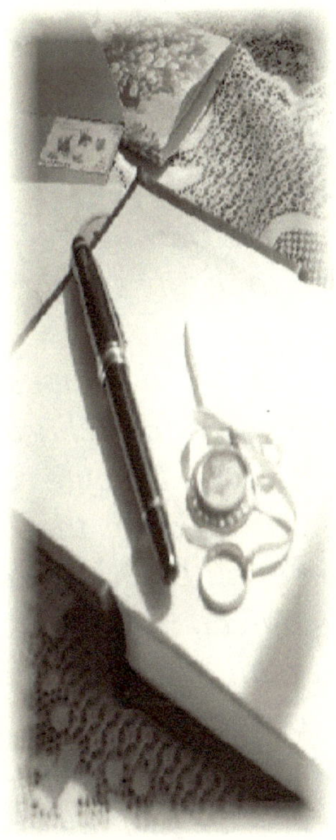

Author's Notes

Some people ask me if Olivia Foxworthy is real. In truth, some are convinced I am keeping Olivia's true identity a secret.

Not all of us find the courage Olivia's faith seemed to amply supply, but we wish for it.

In keeping with the idea that so many can relate to a fictitious character, I'd have to say she has become real to many of us and in fact is the culmination of all I hold true and good and magical.

I believe we, all of us are on an incredible journey and it's so difficult to be positive when standing at life's dangerous precipice of life altering decisions, facing the unexpected.

I chose to follow in Olivia's footsteps and forge my own journey. I try to be

brave as she is even when odds are not in my favor.
I am not certain where this journey will lead, but so far, Olivia has touched the hearts of many. That makes me feel I am in good company with all the fine people who also can fall in love with life, even when it's difficult.
I take this opportunity to thank all readers who took time out of their busy lives and schedules to read my work.
The only thing I know for certain is that I walk this way but once my friends and I can only hope I have touched the hearts of all I came across upon my journey.
Now go laugh a lot, live well, and smile just because it feels good.

~Alex McLellan

Author, Illustrator, Photographer, and Entrepreneur, Alex McLellan lives in Shelburne, Ontario, Canada, with her loving husband and beautiful Co-Author, Miles, the Cat.

"I write because I have to write. Writing is a compulsion for me, an addiction, an inexplicable power, steeling the imagination, creating a doorway into another world where anything can happen. Who if given a choice would not choose to live in such a world?"

-Alex McLellan

Other Works By This Author Available on Amazon Include:

Children's Books Also Include Coloring Pages

New Book
By Local Author
Alex McLellan
Now Available On
Amazon
Cobwebs & Caviar!

Books Can Be Borrowed From The Shelburne Public Library

Books By Alex McLellan (Kimmi)are also currently available at BookLore in Orangeville, ON. And Cobwebs&Caviar In Shelburne

Contact:

Twitter: @AKMcLellanBooks

Facebook: Alex McLellan Books

Website: alexmclellanbooks.com

Email: alexmclellanbooks@gmail.com

Acknowledgements:

Special Thanks To Nathan Sher for Technical Support & Editing

& Book Cover Layout

Front & Back Cover Photography

By Alex McLellan

Location of Book Cover:

Mono, Ontario, Canada

Layout for book cover with help from

Canva found at httsp://www.canva.co

Special Thanks To My Cousin, Debbie, for inspiring me to embark on book three in this series.

"Olivia's Nanna Gray"

Special Thanks To Nick & Theresa Sangiuliano Who Taught Me To Really See People, and loved me as I love them.

www.ingramcontent.com/pod-product-compliance
Lightning Source LLC
LaVergne TN
LVHW090954080826
845145LV00003B/1007

* 9 7 8 1 9 8 9 8 8 7 0 7 3 *